AMOS & BORIS

AMOS & BORIS

WILLIAM STEIG

PUFFIN

For Maggie and Melinda

PUFFIN BOOKS

UK | USA | Canada | Ireland | Australia
India | New Zealand | South Africa

Puffin Books is part of the Penguin Random House group of companies
whose addresses can be found at global.penguinrandomhouse.com.

www.penguin.co.uk
www.puffin.co.uk
www.ladybird.co.uk

First published in the United States by Farrar, Straus and Giroux 1971
This edition published 2018
001

Copyright © William Steig, 1971
The moral right of the author/illustrator has been asserted

Printed in China

A CIP catalogue record for this book is available from the British Library

ISBN: 978–0–141–37467–3

All correspondence to:
Puffin Books
Penguin Random House Children's
80 Strand, London WC2R 0RL

Amos, a mouse, lived by the ocean. He loved the ocean.
He loved the smell of the sea air. He loved to hear the surf sounds –
the bursting breakers, the backwashes with rolling pebbles.

He thought a lot about the ocean, and he wondered about the faraway places on the other side of the water. One day he started building a boat on the beach. He worked on it in the daytime, while at night he studied navigation.

When the boat was finished, he loaded it with cheese, biscuits, acorns, honey, wheat germ, two barrels of fresh water, a compass, a sextant, a telescope, a saw, a hammer and nails and some wood in case repairs should be necessary, a needle and thread for the mending of torn sails, and various other necessities such as bandages and iodine, a yo-yo and playing cards.

On the sixth of September, with a very calm sea, he waited till the high tide had almost reached his boat; then, using his most savage strength, he just managed to push the boat into the water, climb on board, and set sail.

The *Rodent*, for that was the boat's name, proved to be very well made and very well suited to the sea. And Amos, after one miserable day of seasickness, proved to be a natural sailor, very well suited to the ship.

He was enjoying his trip immensely. It was beautiful weather. Day and night he moved up and down, up and down, on waves as big as mountains, and he was full of wonder, full of enterprise, and full of love for life.

One night, in a phosphorescent sea, he marvelled at the sight of some whales spouting luminous water; and later, lying on the deck of his boat gazing at the immense, starry sky, the tiny mouse Amos, a little speck of a living thing in the vast living universe, felt thoroughly akin to it all. Overwhelmed by the beauty and mystery of everything, he rolled over and over and right off the deck of his boat and into the sea.

"Help!" he squeaked as he grabbed desperately at the *Rodent.*
But it evaded his grasp and went bowling along under full sail,
and he never saw it again.

And there he was! Where? In the middle of the immense ocean, a thousand miles from the nearest shore, with no one else in sight as far as the eye could see and not even so much as a stick of driftwood to hold on to. "Should I try to swim home?" Amos wondered. "Or should I just try to stay afloat?" He might swim a mile, but never a thousand. He decided to just keep afloat, treading water and hoping that something – who knows what? – would turn up to save him. But what if a shark, or some big fish, a horse mackerel, turned up? What was he supposed to do to protect himself? He didn't know.

Morning came, as it always does. He was getting terribly tired. He was a very small, very cold, very wet and worried mouse. There was still nothing in sight but the empty sea. Then, as if things weren't bad enough, it began to rain.

At last the rain stopped and the noonday sun gave him a bit of cheer and warmth in the vast loneliness; but his strength was giving out. He began to wonder what it would be like to drown. Would it take very long? Would it feel just awful? Would his soul go to heaven? Would there be other mice there?

As he was asking himself these dreadful questions, a huge head burst through the surface of the water and loomed up over him. It was a whale. "What sort of fish are you?" the whale asked. "You must be one of a kind!"

"I'm not a fish," said Amos. "I'm a mouse, which is a mammal, the highest form of life. I live on land."

"Holy clam and cuttlefish!" said the whale. "I'm a mammal myself, though I live in the sea. Call me Boris," he added.

Amos introduced himself and told Boris how he came to be there in the middle of the ocean. The whale said he would be happy to take Amos to the Ivory Coast of Africa, where he happened to be headed anyway, to attend a meeting of whales from all the seven seas. But Amos said he'd had enough adventure to last him a while. He wanted only to get back home and hoped the whale wouldn't mind going out of his way to take him there.

"Not only would I not mind," said Boris, "I would consider it a privilege. What other whale in all this world ever had the chance to get to know such a strange creature as you! Please climb aboard." And Amos got on Boris's back.

"Are you sure you're a mammal?" Amos asked. "You smell more like a fish." Then Boris the whale went swimming along, with Amos the mouse on his back.

What a relief to be so safe, so secure again! Amos lay down
in the sun, and being worn to a frazzle, he was soon asleep.

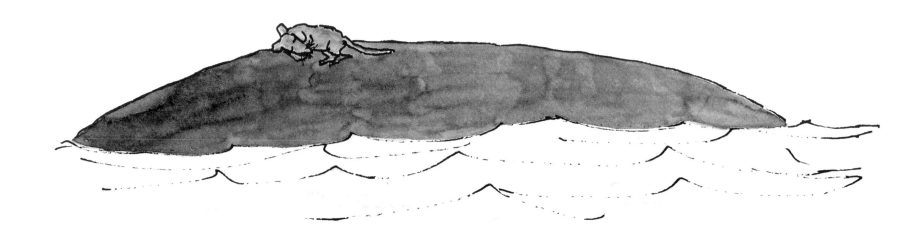

Then all of a sudden he was in the water again, wide awake, spluttering and splashing about! Boris had forgotten for a moment that he had a passenger on his back and had sounded. When he realised his mistake, he surfaced so quickly that Amos was sent somersaulting, tail over whiskers, high into the air.

Hitting the water hurt. Crazy with rage, Amos screamed and punched at Boris until he remembered he owed his life to the whale and quietly climbed on his back. From then on, whenever Boris wanted to sound, he warned Amos in advance and got his okay, and whenever he sounded, Amos took a swim.

Swimming along, sometimes at great speed, sometimes slowly
and leisurely, sometimes resting and exchanging ideas, sometimes
stopping to sleep, it took them a week to reach Amos's home shore.
During that time, they developed a deep admiration for one another.
Boris admired the delicacy, the quivering daintiness, the light touch,
the small voice, the gemlike radiance of the mouse. Amos admired
the bulk, the grandeur, the power, the purpose, the rich voice, and
the abounding friendliness of the whale.

They became the closest possible friends. They told each other about their lives, their ambitions. They shared their deepest secrets with each other. The whale was very curious about life on land and was sorry that he could never experience it. Amos was fascinated by the whale's accounts of what went on deep under the sea. Amos sometimes enjoyed running up and down on the whale's back for exercise. When he was hungry, he ate plankton. The only thing he missed was fresh, unsalty water.

The time came to say goodbye. They were at the shore. "I wish we could be friends forever," said Boris. "We *will* be friends forever, but we can't be together. You must live on land and I must live at sea. I'll never forget *you*, though."

"And you can be sure I'll never forget you," said Amos. "I will always be grateful to you for saving my life and I want you to remember that if you ever need my help I'd be more than glad to give it!" How he could ever possibly help Boris, Amos didn't know, but he knew how willing he was.

The whale couldn't take Amos all the way in to land. They said their last goodbye and Amos dived off Boris's back and swam to the sand.

From the top of a cliff he watched Boris spout twice and disappear. Boris laughed to himself. "How could that little mouse ever help me? Little as he is, he's all heart. I love him, and I'll miss him terribly."

Boris went to the conference off the Ivory Coast of Africa and then went back to a life of whaling about, while Amos returned to his life of mousing around. And they were both happy.

Many years after the incidents just described, when Amos was no longer a very young mouse, and when Boris was no longer a very young whale, there occurred one of the worst storms of the century,

Hurricane Yetta; and it just so happened that Boris
the whale was flung ashore by a tidal wave and stranded on the
very shore where Amos happened to make his home.

It also just so happened that when the storm had cleared up and Boris was lying high and dry on the sand, losing his moisture in the hot sun and needing desperately to be back in the water, Amos came down to the beach to see how much damage Hurricane Yetta had done. Of course Boris and Amos recognised each other at once. I don't have to tell you how these old friends felt at meeting again in this desperate situation. Amos rushed toward Boris. Boris could only look at Amos.

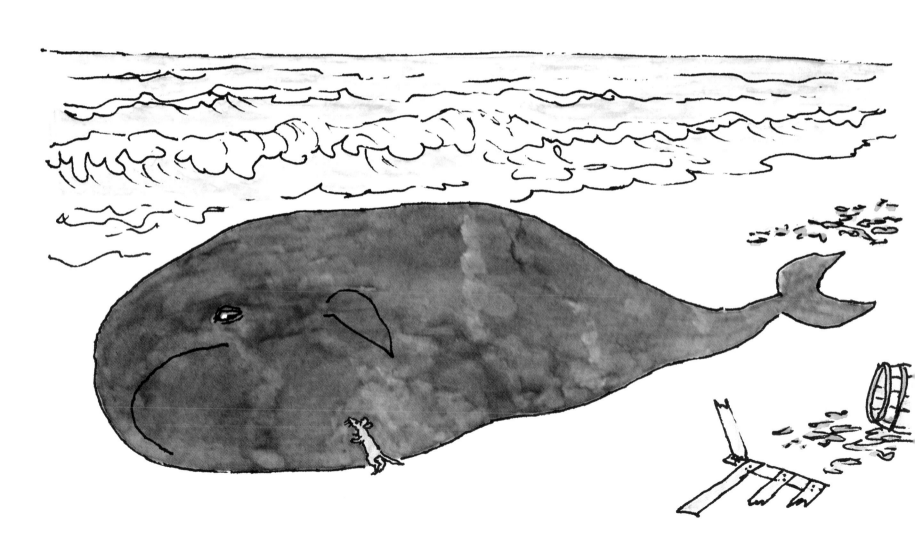

"Amos, help me," said the mountain of a whale to the mote of a mouse. "I think I'll die if I don't get back in the water soon." Amos gazed at Boris in an agony of pity. He realised he had to do something very fast and had to think very fast about what it was he had to do. Suddenly he was gone.

"I'm afraid he won't be able to help me," said Boris to himself. "Much as he wants to do something, what can such a little fellow do?"

Just as Amos had once felt, all alone in the middle of the ocean, Boris felt now, lying alone on the shore. He was sure he would die. And just as he was preparing to die, Amos came racing back with two of the biggest elephants he could find.

Without wasting time, these two good-hearted elephants got to pushing with all their might at Boris's huge body until he began turning over, breaded with sand, and rolling down toward the sea. Amos, standing on the head of one of the elephants, yelled instructions, but no one heard him.

In a few minutes Boris was already in water, with waves washing at him, and he was feeling the wonderful wetness. "You have to be *out* of the sea really to know how good it is to be *in* it," he thought. "That is, if you're a whale." Soon he was able to wiggle and wriggle into deeper water.

He looked back at Amos on the elephant's head. Tears were
rolling down the great whale's cheeks. The tiny mouse had tears
in his eyes too. "Goodbye, dear friend," squeaked Amos.
"Goodbye, dear friend," rumbled Boris, and he disappeared in
the waves. They knew they might never meet again. They knew
they would never forget each other.